Food +
Farming

Baker Cat

To Sam, Billy and Isobel

BAKER CAT
A JONATHAN CAPE BOOK 0 224 07004 5

Published in Great Britain by Jonathan Cape,
an imprint of Random House Children's Books

This edition published 2004

1 3 5 7 9 10 8 6 4 2

Copyright © Posy Simmonds, 2004

RANDOM HOUSE CHILDREN'S BOOKS
61–63 Uxbridge Road, London W5 5SA
A division of The Random House Group Ltd
RANDOM HOUSE AUSTRALIA (PTY) LTD
20 Alfred Street, Milsons Point, Sydney,
New South Wales 2061, Australia
RANDOM HOUSE NEW ZEALAND LTD
18 Poland Road, Glenfield, Auckland 10, New Zealand
RANDOM HOUSE (PTY) LTD
Endulini, 5A Jubilee Road, Parktown 2193, South Africa

THE RANDOM HOUSE GROUP Limited Reg. No. 954009
www.kidsatrandomhouse.co.uk

A CIP catalogue record for this book is available from the British Library.

Printed in China

POSY SIMMONDS

Baker Cat

A Tom Maschler Book

JONATHAN CAPE • LONDON

There was once a cat who belonged to
a mean old baker and his lazy wife.
The cat must have had a name, but
nobody really knew what it was.
The baker called him:
"Useless!"
"Cloth-ears!"
"Mangy fur-bag!"

The baker's wife couldn't bear cats and kept one only because the bakery was plagued with mice. Mice gave her the screaming shudders.

The cat was made to do all the work. Every day, while the baker sat grumbling and shouting, the cat scurried to and fro . . .

stopping mouseholes . . .   mixing dough . . .

peeling, slicing . . .   rolling, icing . . .   chasing mice . . .

setting traps . . .

baking bread . . .

washing up . . .

sweeping up . . .

and, finally, shutting up the shop.

Then, every night, without so much as a scrap of supper, the cat was shooed into the storeroom.

Go on! Earn your keep! Catch those mice!

You show me plenty of mouse tails in the morning and I'll show you a good breakfast!

You know the deal: The bigger your catch, the bigger your meal!

Tired out from his long day, the cat was never a match for the rude and frisky mice.

Cloth-ears!

Mangy fur-bag!

In the morning he seldom had any mouse tails to show the baker.

As a result, his breakfasts grew mingier and mingier.

The poor over-worked cat grew thin and tired and very tearful.

The mice felt sorry for the cat.
They held a meeting and made a plan.

While the cat had a good sleep, the mice went and borrowed some things from the shop round the corner.

In the morning the baker bellowed ...

Every night for several nights, the mice repeated their plan.
While the cat slept soundly, they produced huge numbers of mouse tails . . .

and every morning the baker
was obliged to reward the cat with
larger and larger breakfasts.

The baker and his wife couldn't really grumble.

As for the mice, left in peace in the storeroom, they held ENORMOUS parties for all their families, friends and relations.

Everything was just fine ... until the day the baker ordered the cat to make thirty meringues, forty jam tarts and four dozen walnut brownies. When the cat went to the storeroom he found ...

All afternoon, the baker stamped and roared ...

It was time for another plan . . .

As darkness fell, there were sounds of whispering
and hurrying and scurrying in the street
outside the bakery . . .

and all night long, behind the storeroom door there
was a skittering and scuttering and a chorus of tiny squeaks:
"This way, that way, wind the wool, this way, that way, together – PULL!"

In the morning the baker roared . . .

What d'you mean there was **no** sugar?!

There was tons of it! **No sugar** indeed!

Show me!

Eeuuk!

And so they did. And they never came back.

"What are you going to do now, Cat?" said the mice.

"Keep shop," said the cat, "that's what."

"You'll have to put your name on the shop," said the mice.
"But we still don't know what it is . . ."